For Steve.
"Shyness is nice,
but shyness can stop you."
Beth Bracken

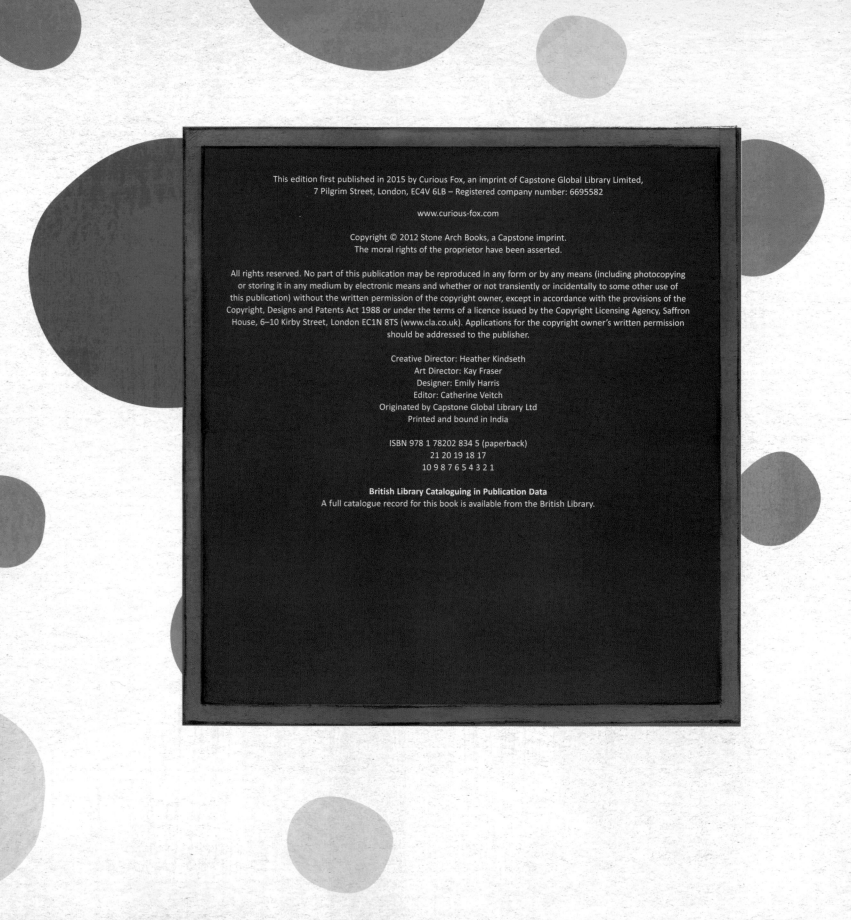

This edition first published in 2015 by Curious Fox, an imprint of Capstone Global Library Limited, 7 Pilgrim Street, London, EC4V 6LB – Registered company number: 6695582

www.curious-fox.com

Creative Director: Heather Kindseth
Art Director: Kay Fraser
Designer: Emily Harris
Editor: Catherine Veitch
Originated by Capstone Global Library Ltd
Printed and bound in India

ISBN 978 1 78202 834 5 (paperback)
21 20 19 18 17
10 9 8 7 6 5 4 3 2 1

British Library Cataloguing in Publication Data
A full catalogue record for this book is available from the British Library.

Too Shy for Show and Tell

written by Beth Bracken   illustrated by Jennifer Bell

Curious Fox
a capstone company-publishers for children

Sam was a quiet boy.
Nobody knew much about him.

Sam loved playing with lorries and cars, but nobody knew that.

Sam's favourite food was chocolate cake,
but nobody knew that.

Sam thought dogs were the best animals in the world,
but nobody knew that, either.

The only thing that people knew about Sam was that
he didn't talk much.

And Sam really didn't like talking in front of people,
which is why Sam hated show and tell.

On Wednesday, Miss Ostrich told the class that show and tell would be on Friday.

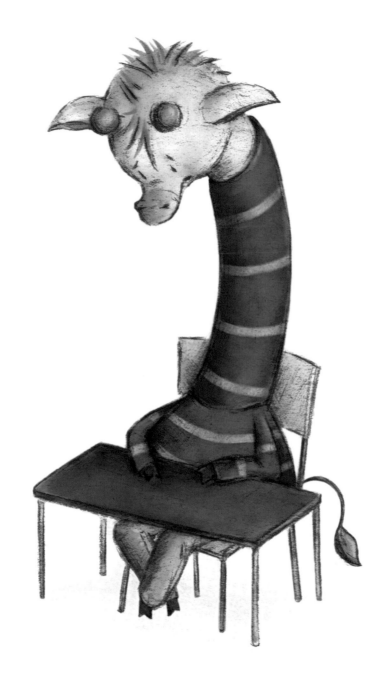

Sam spent most of Thursday worrying. He had a great thing to bring for show and tell, but he was scared.

On Friday, Sam didn't get out of bed.

"My tummy hurts," he lied.

"You're fine, and you need to go to school today," his mum said.

At school, Sam told Miss Ostrich he'd forgotten about show and tell.

"I didn't bring anything," he said. But that wasn't true.
His perfect show and tell thing was in his rucksack.

"That's okay," Miss Ostrich said. "You can just tell the class about the thing you left at home."

Sam was terrified. He didn't want to talk in front of everyone.
The thought of it made his tummy hurt really, really bad.

He imagined that he'd say something silly.

Or that he'd mess up his words.

Or that he'd faint.

Or that he'd cry.

Sam watched the other children show their show and tell things.

Cameron showed some socks that his grandma had knitted him.
Everyone clapped when he had finished.

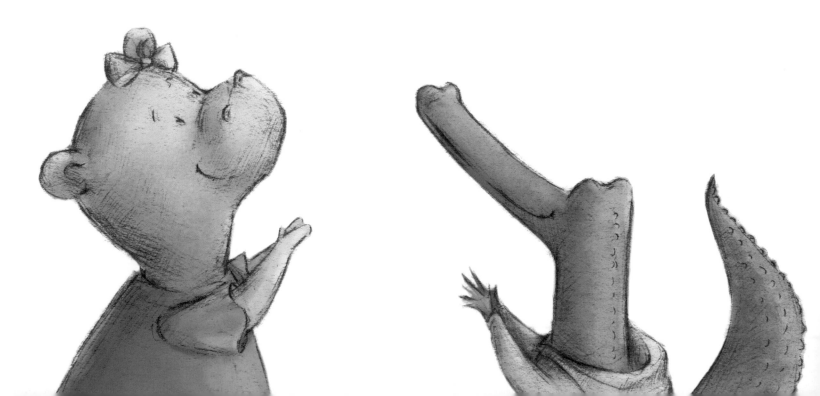

Helena showed a new doll she had for her birthday.
Everyone clapped when she had finished.

Alex showed a cool leaf that he found on the way to school.

Alex said "weaf" instead of "leaf," but nobody seemed to notice, and everyone clapped when he had finished.

Then it was Sam's turn. He took his perfect show and tell thing out of his rucksack and went to the front of the class.

"What do you have to show us today, Sam?"
Miss Ostrich asked with a smile.

Sam took a deep breath. He looked at his classmates.
They were quietly waiting.

Sam held up his picture. "This is my new dog," he said. "I named him Chocolate, because that's my favourite kind of cake, and he's the colour of chocolate cake."

Sam didn't faint.

He didn't mess up his words.

He didn't cry.

And no one laughed.

Instead, everyone clapped
when he had finished.

Now everyone in the class knew
a little bit more about Sam.

Next time, he thought,
I'll bring my biggest fire engine.

And he did.